Augustus Bozzi Granville

The Sumbul

Anatiposi

Augustus Bozzi Granville

The Sumbul

Reprint of the original.

1st Edition 2023 | ISBN: 978-3-38230-496-6

Anatiposi Verlag is an imprint of Outlook Verlagsgesellschaft mbH.

Verlag (Publisher): Outlook Verlag GmbH, Zeilweg 44, 60439 Frankfurt, Deutschland
Vertretungsberechtigt (Authorized to represent): E. Roepke, Zeilweg 44, 60439 Frankfurt, Deutschland
Druck (Print): Books on Demand GmbH, In de Tarpen 42, 22848 Norderstedt, Deutschland

THE SUMBUL.

THE SUMBUL:

A NEW ASIATIC REMEDY

OF GREAT POWER

AGAINST

NERVOUS DISORDERS, SPASMS OF THE STOMACH, CRAMP,
HYSTERICAL AFFECTIONS,
PARALYSIS OF THE LIMBS, AND EPILEPSY;

WITH AN

ACCOUNT OF ITS PHYSICAL, CHEMICAL, AND MEDICINAL CHARACTERS,
AND SPECIFIC PROPERTY OF CHECKING THE PROGRESS
OF COLLAPSE-CHOLERA, AS FIRST ASCERTAINED
IN RUSSIA.

BY

A. B. GRANVILLE, M.D., F.R.S., V.P.O.S.

OF THE ROYAL COLLEGE OF PHYSICIANS, LONDON,
&c. &c. &c.

SECOND EDITION.

LONDON:
JOHN CHURCHILL, NEW BURLINGTON STREET.
1859.

NOTICE.

In the course of a long practice in London, both as an obstetric and as a general physician, it has been my good fortune to introduce for the first time into the Materia Medica of this country two or three new remedies, which, received at first with hesitation and even incredulity, were nevertheless, in the course of time, accepted generally by the profession. They are now standard medicinal agents, admitted into the Pharmacopœias of both England and Scotland. I allude to prussic acid,* the counter-irritating lotions, and the stimulating alkaline drops.†

By a singular coincidence of circumstances, I am now enabled to add another equally and entirely new remedy, the "SUMBUL," totally unknown either as a

---

* First introduced by the writer, in 1815, through the *London Medical Repository*, and afterwards in a treatise on the subject, in 1819–20, which went through two editions.

† The composition and properties of both are given at full length in the *Lancet*, No. VI., for October, 1838.

medicinal drug or as an ordinary substance to the
profession in England. Nor was its existence better
known on the Continent until a very recent date,
and then only partially, although it was there first
employed as a remedy. And yet the indisputable
powers which the Sumbul has displayed under
proper guidance, would seem to demand for such a
remedial agent a larger field of publicity.

This I have undertaken to give it in the following
pages.

109, *Piccadilly,*
    30*th May,* 1850.

P.S.—A re-issue of this slender production being
called for, I have added a few facts and observations
calculated to make the history of this new and remarkable medicinal agent more complete.

No. 1, *Curzon-street, Mayfair,*
    31*st March,* 1859.

CONTENTS.

THE SUMBUL.

I. *History of the Drug.*

Sumbul is the Asiatic name of a vegetable drug, hitherto nearly altogether unknown to the medical practitioners of Europe. It is only within the last ten years that in some parts of the Continent it acquired considerable celebrity, in consequence of its ascertained value in the worst stages of Cholera. The physicians of Moscow and St. Petersburg, who, from their greater proximity to the locality whence the drug is derived, were among the first to bring the Sumbul into use as a remedy against that terrible disorder, hesitate not to ascribe to its virtues the saving of thousands of lives during the epidemic of 1849.

But previously to such an application of the drug, the Sumbul had been employed in Russia, as a stimulant and a rouser of animal energy in the advanced stages of malignant fevers (Typhus), as well as in dysentery of an asthenic or debilitating character, not less than in chronic diarrhœa, with unquestionable success.

In a letter written from Kissingen to the Editor of the *Times* late in July, 1849, and inserted in that journal of the 8th of August, giving an account of

the method of treating Cholera in the civil and
military hospitals both of Moscow and St. Petersburg,
as witnessed by myself in a recent professional visit
to both capitals, I pointed out the comparative successful result obtained by that method, in the ac-
companying official returns of attacks, deaths, and
recoveries in cases of Cholera in certain hospitals.
That method I described as both simple and new—
and then it was that I first named the Sumbul as
one of the agents in the method in question. At
the time of so naming that drug, I surmised that
it might be a well-known agent among my brother
practitioners in England—and I confess I expected
to find, on my return to this country, the Russian
method and Russian remedy in full operation.

The contrary, however, proved to be the case, and
the Russian mode of treating Cholera did not attract
the attention it unquestionably deserved.

The letter describing that mode had indeed been
copied from the *Times* into three or four other English journals, and also in the *Galignani* of Paris. It
was quoted and favourably commented upon by the
Medical Gazette, and the *Pharmaceutical Journal* of
London; but I was never able to discover that any
attempt had been made by English medical practitioners to give the system a trial, or to become
acquainted with the medicine.

And yet the signal failure of all the methods of
cure then employed in England, numerous, multifarious, and contradictory as they were, and which
did not prevent the weekly number of 823 deaths
in the metropolis on the 11th of August, 1849, to

swell into a weekly one of 2026 on the 12th of September following,* might have suggested the propriety of trying a new mode of treatment which came recommended by sufficient success officially proclaimed.

Further inquiries, however, soon showed me that this course could not have been adopted in England, for the Sumbul—which was the one remedy to be employed in the new mode in question of treating the disease, and which I had assumed to be possibly a well-known substance in the pharmacy of this country—proved in reality to be wholly and entirely unknown in England.

This I ascertained to be a fact by making personal inquiries of some of our principal chemists and druggists, as well as of the superintendent at Apothecaries' Hall—to all of whom I exhibited large specimens of the drug I had brought with me, and allowed them to examine it. No one, however, seemed to recognise it as a former acquaintance, either in substance or in name. And when recourse was had to all the best English works on Materia Medica, we found the same total absence of all information or knowledge of that substance. The only allusion to the Sumbul we could discover in any English publication was that made by Dr. Pereira, in the *Pharmaceutical Journal* for 1848, where he simply reports that he had received such a substance, together with some other drugs, from St. Petersburg, adding, that Dr. Martiny of Darmstadt had employed it with success in Dropsies.

* See Registrar-General's Report.

But although neither Mr. Savory, nor Mr. Redwood of the Pharmaceutical Society, nor the gentleman at Apothecaries' Hall, could recognise the drug, they all agreed and admitted, that, judging from its peculiar taste and strong perfume, they considered it as likely to be endowed with potent properties.

Convinced at that time, and still more so now, (since personal experience has come to my aid,) that whether for the treatment of that scourge, the Cholera, or of any analogous disorder, this powerful new agent, the Sumbul, must now take its proper rank in the materia medica of Europe, and consequently of England, I proceed to relate the additional information I have succeeded in obtaining since I first introduced the subject into the columns of the *Times*. This I am enabled to do, not only from living authorities and books, but also from personal observation and professional experience, in the course of the last ten years.

To complete this brief history of the drug, it is right to mention that Mr. Savory, anxious to possess himself of a medicinal substance of which I had spoken to him in such exalted terms, and having learned from what source I had procured the specimens I had brought with me, wrote to a friend at St. Petersburg for both the drug and some account of it, at two different times, without obtaining the latter, and only some inferior specimens of the former. Not at all discouraged by this disappointment, and Hamburgh having been named by me as a most likely place in which to find the Sumbul, inasmuch as there were two among my own specimens obtained from thence, Mr. Savory applied in that quarter for, and was able to obtain, a sufficient quantity of the drug, for which I am informed he was made to pay a high price. But no information concerning the substance itself could he get along with it, except that it was used in perfumery. He next endeavoured, therefore, to procure what knowledge he could by inquiries among the botanists and scientific medical men in London—one of whom, in particular, well known for his industry and persevering researches among books, had offered to lay a wager he would succeed in obtaining the desired information. But neither through this gentleman nor through any other channel has Mr. Savory been able to attain his object.

Mr. Savory has, nevertheless, worked upon the materials he had procured from Hamburgh and whatever information I had originally given him in September last, when I first exhibited the substance to him. He has produced one or two preparations from the drug, one of which, a tincture in proof spirits, he afterwards propounded to one of the medical officers of King's College Hospital as a likely remedy to be of use in Epilepsy, a suggestion he derived from the drug bearing in one of its physical characters some analogy to musk, as will be seen by a reference to the second number of the *Lancet* for January, 1850.*

* The late eminent botanist, Robert Brown, informed me afterwards that he had specimens of the Sumbul given him by Dr. Richter, at Moscow, in 1832, which he brought to England, and that the same gentleman had sent him some more specimens, still in his possession, but unaccompanied

On my own part I lost not a moment in availing myself of the possession of a quantity of the Sumbul which had been presented to me by the medical staff of the Petro-Paulowsky Hospital, in St. Petersburg, in the month of July, 1849—and of the information I had obtained respecting it in Russia, as well as subsequently in some parts of Germany immediately before my return home. I set about making various preparations of it, both as infusions and decoctions of various strength, from which I collected solid precipitates for examination—next as tinctures, with alcohol and ether, singly or conjointly—also as an extract, and in powder, all of which preparations I have had opportunities of employing in practice, ever since September last, in cases of disordered nerves and such other analogous complaints as are mentioned in the title-page, among which Epilepsy is reckoned as one. The coincidence of Mr. Savory having, from fair and logical deductions, suggested it also as a likely remedy for that disease, and the success which has attended its use in that case, as well as in other cases of that complaint which came under my own observation, may be accepted as an encouraging circumstance in the useful application to be made of this drug.

I also employed a respectable chemist to make an ethereal alcoholic tincture of the Sumbul, with some of my own specimens, which cannot be otherwise than most genuine, considering the quarter

by any account of their nature and properties, or any other information respecting the substance, which had been lying by him unnoticed ever since.

they came from; and it has proved so powerful, that the operator, who tasted it, acknowledged it to be extraordinary in its effects on the mouth and palate.

At Heidelberg, in the warehouse of one of the most extensive importers of medicinal drugs in Germany, I found, in August last, with Professor Pfeuffer, a small quantity of Sumbul under that name. The specimens were very old, and had been obtained from Hamburgh; but how long before, none could tell. They looked different from those I had brought from Russia, and I have been informed very lately by the learned professor, that when employed, as I had suggested at the time, in the cholera at Manheim, they proved inert. Upon the Heidelberg druggist writing to St. Petersburg for a fresh supply, he was apprized that such a vast quantity had been consumed during the late epidemic in the two Russian capitals, that it would be difficult to procure any until a fresh importation.

This statement completes all that has been ascertained of the history of this new remedy in England, as communicated by myself in the letter addressed to the *Times*, to which I have referred, and in the present publication.

II. *Description of the Sumbul; its Birthplace;*
its Physical Characters.

The SUMBUL does not consist, as on a first appearance I fancied, and stated in my former announcement, of a mass of roots and leaves of a greenish plant bruised and pressed together.* The mistake arose from my being shown at first, at St. Petersburg, a mass of the substance which had been previously bruised together with the remains of a strong decoction of the same that had a greenish colour. The Sumbul, on the contrary, is a single, thick, homogeneous root, from two to three and even four inches diameter, circular sections of which, having a yellowish-white fibrous look, and from an inch to an inch and a half in depth, are brought into the Russian drug market at Moscow, through Kiatka, from the centre of Asia.

Bucharia, a district to the north of Mount Thibet and part of the Mongol Empire, is considered by the botanists Ermann and Von Ledebour to be the *habitat* of the plant which furnishes this root. Others, on the contrary, think it the produce of Trebisond, and not a few are inclined to ascribe to Persia the birthplace of the Sumbul. The latter individuals are people who deal in drugs.

The Nuremberg druggists, Hagen and Co., for example, believe the *habitat* of the original plant not to be known. They are disposed to consider Trebisond, Constantinople, and Nidjü-Novgorod, to be the most likely places from whence it is derived.

All these discrepancies of opinion among wholesale

---

* It is a curious fact, that on my first exhibiting one of the specimens of the root to Mr. Robert Brown, at the British Museum, on the 14th of May, (1850,) that eminent botanist was at first inclined to doubt whether it was a genuine root, and not rather a congeries of roots, until he carefully explored a fresh section of it with the magnifying lens.

drug merchants are easily reconcilable, and lead to the conclusion that their authority is not to be put in competition with, still less should it supersede, the deliberate opinion of botanists and travellers, such as those I have alluded to in a preceding paragraph.

That some people should have deemed Persia to be the birthplace of the Sumbul is not surprising, seeing that the substance is much used in that country as a remedy against mephitic or depressing exhalations, especially in mines. We may equally explain the reason for the other opinion, which gives to Constantinople, Trebisond, or Nidjü-Novgorod, the merit of producing the drug in question. These are places of export for all Asiatic produce, and there the Sumbul will ever be found on sale. This constant presence of the drug in those localities has induced drug merchants to imagine it to be one of their products, instead of being an importation.

Moreover, in Persia and in Constantinople the use of perfumes, such as the Sumbul possesses in an eminent degree, is in great vogue. Its employment, therefore, in those parts, for the purpose of extracting its perfume, may be very considerable, and would lead to the conclusion that the plant which yields the perfume itself is indigenous.*

---

* From Dr. Royle's "Illustrations of the Botany of the Himalayan Mountains," we learn that the name of *Sunbul*, pronounced Sumbul, designates, in Oriental language, three or four different vegetable products ; none of which, however, can possibly be the substance under consideration, as from the description of their roots the difference between the former and the latter is most complete. But this information of Dr. Royle may serve to explain why such a variety of opinions

There is every reason to believe that our root belongs to a plant of the umbelliferous family, probably an aquatic plant, or at least a lover of humid soils and the banks of rivers. When fresh, the root must be very considerable in size, inasmuch as though it reaches us in its dried state and much compressed, yet it exhibits specimens of the thickness of four inches in diameter, some of which I have had in my own possession. But these specimens vary in form as well as size, some of them assuming the shape of a tuberous, others of a fusiform root, without, however, any of the fibrils which accompany those kinds of roots. I have met with some samples which looked like the root of white hellebore in form; others, again, which had the appearance of being arranged in concentric circles.

In all specimens observed, the epidermis or external covering is generally dusky, or of a light brown; when of a darker colour it is a token of old age. The epidermis is very thin and much wrinkled. The inner substance is composed of coarse irregular fibres, which may be readily torn one from the other the moment the external covering is removed, and which constitute a porous texture indicative of its aquatic existence.

When the root is denuded of its external coat, and cut transversely, we observe an external lamina, white and spotted, and an inner one much thicker,

should exist in regard to the natural birthplace of our *Sumbul;* for the name seems to be a generic one, and to have been applied to more than one species of sweet-smelling plant, supposed to be the *Nard,* or "Spikenard" of the ancients.

and yellow. Seen through a magnifying lens, translucid points may be discerned, which have the appearance of starch.*

Two very striking and remarkable physical characters attract attention when we examine this root —first, its perfume, which as nearly as possible approaches to that of the purest musk ; and next, the powerful aroma it exhales in the mouth when masticated.

It was by some people, slightly acquainted with the true characteristics of this substance, conjectured that the smell of musk was not inherent in the drug, but was a mere accession to it, from the drug having probably been packed in bales with other drugs from Asia, of which musk formed a part. But such a supposition is disproved, by the Sumbul retaining its musky odour, however old; by the fact that when a specimen which has lost its original perfume is broken, the perfume immediately appears again from its interior; by the extraction of the said perfume from the root through chemical manipulation ; and, lastly, by the name of *moschus-wurzel* which it has received from some of the continental botanists. This smell of musk is a distinguishing and permanent character in the drug, and readily adheres to the paper or other substance on which it has been laid, or otherwise put in contact with.

Nor is the taste less remarkable, although in the

---

* These shining particles are discernible by the naked eye when a portion of the root is carefully sawed through with a joiner's fine saw ; in that state, the cut surface may not inaptly be compared to a slice of pine-apple.

dry state in which the root reaches Europe, a considerable portion of its sapid properties must have been lost. From the latter cause, no doubt, the taste is not very distinguishable at once. The first impression is that of a feeble sweetness, but this soon ceases, to be succeeded by another—a balsamic impression on the tongue, followed by a bitterish taste by no means unpleasant. Presently, a sharp aroma, as we proceed with the mastication of the drug, develops itself throughout the mouth and throat, imparting a warm feeling to the mouth and fragrance to the breath. In its flavour, it reminds one of Angelica Root, which is the substance that most nearly resembles the Sumbul in some of its physical characters, though not in energy or medicinal properties.

The flavour of the Sumbul is of course greatly heightened by its solution in any spirit; and Mr. Savory related an anecdote to me of a medical man being made to taste a very few drops of its tincture, who after some seconds expressed a lively apprehension lest he had taken something wrong, so potent was the gradual development of the stimulating aroma in his mouth. In not a few instances among my patients, and a few amateurs who wished to try the flavour of the ethereal tincture of Sumbul I prepared, the same expressions of surprise at its peculiar impressions on the tongue were used.

But in this respect it is right to state that the peculiar aromatic flavour here alluded to in chewing the dry root, or its powder, varies considerably in certain specimens, those that appeared the oldest

giving out much less of it than more recent specimens, and those I brought from St. Petersburg
much more than those I procured in Germany from
Hamburgh ; and yet I could not affirm that when
converted into tinctures I could detect any material
difference between the two kinds of specimens in
regard to their balsamic and aromatized flavour.

III. *Chemical and Pharmaceutical Peculiarities of
the Sumbul.*

It is curious how consistent the physical characters of a vegetable substance, endowed with marked
remedial powers, are with its chemical peculiarities,
made out by subsequent analytical examination, or,
as we might call it, by "chemical dissection."

In the present case, this harmony or consistency
between the two is especially striking, and we shall
find that every one of the features of the Sumbul
root detailed in the preceding section is accounted
for by the presence of corresponding chemical principles or bases in its composition.

The chemical analysis of the Sumbul has engaged
the serious attention of two or three eminent organic
chemists in Germany. Dr. Reinsch, Dr. Schnitzlein,
Dr. Frichinger, and Kalthofer, may be mentioned as
the principal investigators. I shall briefly state the
results of their labours, without, however, entering
into the minutiæ of quantitative analysis, which for
medicinal purposes are not in the least essential, but
which would, on the contrary, embarrass the reader
in his clearer understanding and appreciation of the
subject.

According to Dr. Reinsch's analysis, the Sumbul root contains, besides water, traces of an ethereal oil, two balsamic ingredients (resins), one of which is soluble in ether, the other in alcohol; also wax, aromatic spirit, and a bitter substance, soluble both in water and alcohol.

The solution of this bitter substance, when treated with lime and muriate of soda, throws down a sediment consisting of gum, starch, and saline matter.

The balsam seems more particularly to be the seat of the musk-like perfume, which comes out stronger and more distinctly by being wetted with water. Dissolved in ether, it resembles in appearance, consistency, and colour, the balsam of copaiva, and possesses a burning aromatic taste, with a faint, musk-like smell, which, however, is more largely developed by agitating the solution in water. By distillation it gives out a clear yellow peppermint-like tasting oil, having a greenish-white tint; in the retort there remains an indigo-blue coloured mass.

In some more recent experiments, Dr. Reinsch obtained from seventeen ounces of the root an ounce and a half of the balsam, from which he extracted ten grains of a crystallizable acid, to which he has given the name of Sumbulic acid. There is good ground for considering this acid as analogous to Angelic acid, derived from Angelica root. By distilling the balsam, the same chemist procured first a yellowish, and secondly a greenish oil. The former, not unlike Cajeput oil, has a burning taste, smells pleasant and peculiar, and is volatile and very combustible.

Dr. SCHNITZLEIN and Dr. FRICHINGER studied together the chemical properties of the Sumbul root. They examined a beautiful sample of it, consisting of two ounces and six drachms in weight, from a section of the root three inches in diameter. On the cut surface they found a tolerably porous membrane of white colour, incrusted with dirty yellow, in which were discernible parts, which, treated with sulphuric acid, became intensely purple. In other respects, they obtained precisely the same results as Dr. Reinsch.

KALTHOFER made several experiments also with the Sumbul, but more in a pharmaceutical sense. He found the alcoholic tincture to be of a yellowish colour, smelling like musk, and tasting like it, as well as bitter. The ethereal solution is also yellow, tastes sharp on the tongue, with a musk-like perfume. It then leaves behind in the mouth for some time a pungent balsamic taste, like that of the *Imperatoria* plant. By repeated decoction in water, he has observed that the Sumbul throws down a precipitate, which has the appearance of wax.*

By treating some of the root with the nitric acid of commerce, Mr. Barnes, the manager of Mr. Savory's laboratory, has obtained, I understand, a considerable quantity of oxalic acid. Was this evolved or created by the action of the nitric acid? In other words, was it an educt or a product?

* See, for a full chemical description of the Sumbul, BUCH-NER'S *Repert.*, band 33, pp. 25—32; *Pharm. Central Blatt*, 1844, p. 145; also the *Neuesten Entdeckungen in den Materia Medica*, von DIERBACH, band 3; 12th edition; 1847.

With some of the experiments made in Germany my own coincide. I find, for instance, that the alcoholic tincture is rendered thick by a mixture with water, and that the aqueous extract, which is of a yellow-brown colour, does not smell or taste like musk. I have already alluded, also, to the wax-like sediment which I noticed in the strong decoction of the root, and I may add, that a mixture of an alcoholic and of an ethereal tincture does not, like the first of these, become thick upon being mixed with water.

The preceding pharmaceutical preparations of the Sumbul, and some others, may now claim our attention. But here, again, I must premise that I do not profess to enter into the particulars of the several manipulations required of the chemist and druggist in order to obtain those preparations in the best manner; for such is not my present design. We may safely leave these matters in the hands of Mr. Savory, who has been first in the field to procure the root, and has already prepared two alcoholic tinctures of different strength, as well as an extract. Other respectable chemists will not be long in following his example, as soon as sufficient quantities of the drug can be procured. That supply has hitherto been sufficient to afford ample opportunity to a large number of my professional brethren of giving the medicine a trial in their own practice, on the strength of the information herein offered.

In the same manner, as from the physical characters and habits of the Sumbul we are able to predicate the chemical properties it may possess, so can we, once acquainted with the latter, regulate the processes by which pharmaceutical preparations may be obtained.

Thus, looking to the very careful analysis already alluded to by Dr. Reinsch, the pharmaceutist would endeavour, in the first place, to present to the prescribing physician out of this compound substance a solution of both balsams, the one requiring proof spirit, the other ether, so as to have two distinct tinctures. He would also separate the bitter extract, soluble in water, to be administered in the form of pills, while the two former would be used as drops, alone, or in combination with other appropriate substances. Following the same chemical analysis, I should recommend that the ethereal solution of the resinous substance should be made to yield, by distillation, the powerful aromatic oil mentioned by Reinsch and others, to be employed as hereafter to be stated. And lastly, I can add, from my own experience, that a third or compound tincture can be advantageously formed, by mixing two parts of the alcoholic with one part of the ethereal solution, respecting which I shall have to say a word or two further.

Independently of these several official preparations, and the extempore one by decoction or infusion, or both, I may observe that there is every reason for believing that the powdered root, made into the form of pills, or a certain quantity of the fibres of the root masticated, and the saliva swallowed, will prove useful modes of administering this medicine, wherever its prolonged employment is deemed necessary for the cure of certain chronic complaints, in which the Sumbul is indicated.

Speaking, therefore, pharmaceutically, we have the following preparations of the Sumbul equally available in medicine at the discretion of the physician:—1. The root itself masticated. 2. Its impalpable powder, taken as such or in the form of pills. 3. Its infusion in cold water. 4. Its decoction. 5. An aqueous or bitter extract. 6. An alcoholic tincture. 7. An ethereal tincture. 8. A compound tincture. Lastly, An ethereal volatile oil.

IV. *Diseases, for the Cure of which the Sumbul has been Successfully employed.*

It is not the object of the present monograph or memoir on the Sumbul to enter fully into the nature and description of the various maladies for which it has been recommended as a successful remedy. The mere mention of their names will suffice for the professional not less than for the general reader, as such a notice will at once suggest the peculiar character and distinguishing symptoms of the several disorders it denominates. All that can be presented in the remaining pages is to enumerate the diseases in question, and show on what authority, by what experience, and with which of the preparations of the Sumbul, the cures have been effected.

The diseases, then, in which this singular drug has been recommended and employed with success are—

1st. What are commonly called nervous disorders, a very comprehensive class, for which, *à priori,* one would expect such a substance as the Sumbul to be eminently useful.

2ndly. Spasms of the stomach, and cramp.

3rdly. Hysteria, and all the varieties of hysterical affections.

4thly. Chlorosis, amenorrhœa, and dysmenorrhœa.

5thly. Paralysis of the limbs.

6thly. Epilepsy.

7thly. Dropsy.

In a separate section I shall speak of the power of the Sumbul in a much more formidable malady than all the preceding—I mean, Collapse-cholera.

It will immediately strike every reader, that the nervous system seems to be the constituent part of the human frame most susceptible of the action of this new remedy, for of the six classes of disorders here enumerated, five concern entirely and distinctly the nerves of our body. This was to be expected, considering the great and diffusible energy of some of the principal constituents of the Sumbul, its stimulating qualities, and the fragrance and volatility of its more ethereal principles. It was this last consideration, doubtless, that first suggested its employment in the same complaints for which an analogous remedy, the *Angelica* root and *Imperatoria* (*Masterwort*), had been known of old to have been employed with a fair share of success, though of much inferior power.

Dr. Reinsch states, that in nervous atrophy, its efficacy is undoubted; in low or nervous fevers succeeding typhus, Dr. Tillmann and Dr. Richter have employed it for the last thirteen or fourteen years with very marked benefit; while Dr. Martiny, of Darmstadt, has found it beneficial in all those cases of dropsy which depend on impaired nervous orgasm.

I have myself, within the last few months, employed the Sumbul, sometimes in one, and sometimes in another, of its preparations, with immediate benefit, in cases of severe spasms of the stomach, whether arising from flatulency (the prolific parent of many painful disorders and sensations), or from actual cramp in its muscular coats, dependent on nervous irritation, or what the French call "crispation des nerfs." In the case of an elderly lady, who for many successive weeks had been liable to what she used to call "bursts of wind" in the stomach, waking her up in the middle of the night, the employment of the Sumbul, under the form of my own compound ethereal tincture, taken at the moment, with the view to relieve present sufferings, and in the form of powder, as a progressive remedy afterwards, completed the cure in a short time. I have likewise observed an almost instantaneous relief, in an attack of cramp in the stomach, from taking a number of drops of the compound ethereal tincture on a lump or two of sugar. This is the best vehicle, in my opinion, for the extemporaneous administration of this remedy upon any sudden emergency.

A most interesting additional fact I have elicited from my practice, when so employing the tincture in question, that on its energetic influence slowly subsiding, a quiet sleep almost invariably follows.

But the third class of diseases is the one, in the

treatment of which, perhaps, I have found the various preparations of the Sumbul most efficacious. One very recent case, indeed, of regular hysteria, attended with what the patient styled *corkscrew* pains in the left region of the uterus and its appendages, which had long baffled the skill of medical attendants, has afforded me an almost miraculous proof of the efficacy of the Sumbul in hysterical and uterine affections, as the painful sensations subsided very quickly, and finally gave way, to all appearance altogether, in a comparatively short period.

I have at this moment a case of hysterical pain, or spasm (as the mother of the patient calls it), in a young lady, who bore, for more than a year, a gathering or abscess at the head of the psoas muscle, in the right hip, which an eminent city surgeon had not deemed necessary to open, and which broke of itself after repeated applications of poultices, under my direction, discharging a very large quantity of matter. The extension of the latter down the psoas muscle has probably produced irritation of the pelvic and uterine nerves, and given rise to the hysterical or spasmodic attacks alluded to. I directed a number of drops to be given, two or three times a day, of the tincture of Sumbul, and I expect to hear of its having allayed the distressing symptom. The patient is at that age when the derangement of another important function would follow these spasms, should not the Sumbul succeed in removing them.*

* May 16.—The mother has just been to inform me, that after taking the Sumbul drops for two days, the pains ceased;

This leads me to speak of the complaints enumerated under the fourth class, which seem to afford a very fair field for trying the different preparations of the Sumbul. My own experience, in this respect, is limited to one or two cases*—and of course no one else in this country can be quoted as having had any. Accustomed, during many years of obstetrical practice, to view these disorders as not purely nervous, but rather as the effect of congestion and local inflammation, producing those singular results which I described, with many coloured plates, in a former work,† I am not inclined to encourage, still less hastily to employ, diffusible stimuli or energetic excitants, as have been generally recommended in such complaints ; but where torpor or manifest atony of the nervous power exists, I should not hesitate to recommend and use any suitable preparation of the remedy now under consideration. In the two cases alluded to, the one occurring in a married lady who had suffered much from dysmenorrhœa, which was evidently the cause of her low standard of health since her marriage, as well as of her having no children, the decoction, administered once a day only, and the compound tincture drops, every night, in a

since which period the recovery, after a long trial of the medicine, went on regularly though slowly, the abscess never reappearing again. This was written eight years ago, since which time my experience has extended to a larger number of successful cases, with some disappointments.

* This was written in 1850, since which several similar examples have occurred in my practice for the last nine years.

† Graphic Illustrations of Abortion, &c. Plates, 4to. Churchill. 1836.

little milk, accomplished a perfect cure of the disease. The other case was one of chlorosis in a pale and puttyish-faced young woman, indolent of habit, highly nervous, fanciful in her appetite, and hardly ever regular. Here I gave the ethereal tincture, as the most appropriate preparation for the complaint, in almost homœopathic doses ; and the result has been most satisfactory.

Concerning the disease named in the fifth class, and again in epilepsy—the last but one of our division of diseases—I should have much to say were it not that the object of the present pages is to describe and demonstrate the medicinal virtues of the Sumbul, not the nature and intrinsic character of the diseases themselves, against which that remedy has been employed. But as the right employment of the remedy itself requires that we should distinguish the *species*, as it were, of paralysis and epilepsy, to be treated, it is not a matter of choice, but of necessity, that I should distinctly state that we never ought to employ the preparations of Sumbul, in either the one or the other, so long as there is any reason for suspecting the continued presence of vascular fulness, (congestion,) or of inflammation in the cerebellum or any portion of the spinal marrow, the first occurrence of either of which, or of both, was the cause of the original paralytic stroke or of the first epileptic fit.

I am old enough to have seen and conversed, at the Institute of France, with the celebrated Portal, then ninety years of age, and as full of vigour and as clear-headed as if he had been twoscore years younger, on the nature and treatment of epilepsy, on which subject he had published one of the most complete books, acknowledged, ever since, as a standard work. Portal said : Almost all the vaunted remedies against epilepsy are calculated to protract, and even to increase, rather than alleviate or cure, the disease ; for they all assume that the nervous cords are unstrung, and require to be wound up and stimulated ; whereas the real fact is, that the disease continues, or is persisting, because the same state of fulness of the bloodvessels and pressure by them on the cerebral or spinal matter which first occasioned the disease, *are persisting.*

The having lost sight of this doctrine has been the cause of infinite mischief. Hardly any distinction has been made between such a condition of things, in the majority of cases of epilepsy which require local depletion or the abstraction of blood, and that other condition of the disease which demands the use of the most energetic rousers of neurolism. When the latter obtains, the double tincture of Sumbul will be found of immense efficacy ; but it requires care, and management, and perseverance, and it will be found to leave almost all the pre-eulogized heroic anti-epileptic remedies behind. In one case—that of a clergyman, in whom the disease was manifestly spinal, and the attacks of epilepsy (one of which I witnessed, and therefore there can be no mistake about it) were nocturnal and hebdomadal—the *tinctura Sumbuli composita,* prepared first by myself, was persevered in for ten or twelve weeks. The result may be summed up in the few words of the patient himself, contained in a letter to me of April last.

"I take the Sumbul very regularly. The fits have been very, very slight, hardly anything ; they seem to me to be the least part of the complaint, and not sooner on than off."

An unmarried middle-aged lady, whom I had treated with the usual vaunted remedies for cerebellic epilepsy, producing sudden falls forward, with foaming at the mouth, and unconsciousness of any attack having taken place after it was over, willingly submitted to the proposed change of medicine, and took the Sumbul in powder. The attacks became less frequent. They afterwards were shorter in duration ; and at length appear to have left her. She took altogether five hundred grains of the powder, in carefully graduated doses.

Four similar cases have occurred in my practice since the first publication of this essay.

I recollect being shown, many years since, a celebrated anti-epileptic powder, of which a Dutch count was supposed to possess the secret, and in which the smell of angelica and musk was predominant. It had in its time a great vogue ; and, for aught I know, it may still have. Patients used to go from this country to be under the care of this nobleman abroad, for the sake of taking his powder against epileptic fits. Could it have been the *Sumbul* that gave the peculiar perfume to the powder ? If I recollect right, this Dutch nobleman boasted that his ancestors had obtained the secret in India !

The case of epilepsy, alluded to in a previous page,

placed under the care of one of the physicians of King's College Hospital, and quoted in the *Lancet*, is thus reported upon in a memorandum given me by Mr. Savory a few days back :—" J. Webb, locksmith ; epilepsy ; came into the hospital on 2nd March ; has had eight fits in a fortnight. ℞ Tincturæ Sumbuli, ℳxx., ter die sumend. Has taken it regularly to the present time (May 12). Is now an out-patient. Has had no fits for three weeks."

Fresh testimony as to the efficacy of the Sumbul in what I call passive chronic epilepsy, continues to be sent from the country. A medical gentleman from Liverpool says, (June, 1854,) " Upon the whole, I have now obtained a tolerable body of evidence, which is decidedly in favour of Sumbul in cases of epilepsy and chorea ; and I think more highly of the remedy than I expected from the occasional accounts I received from friends before I began really to investigate its claims."

Another communication, from the father of a young man twenty years of age, a builder by profession, and who had, from the age of twelve, been subject to epileptic fits every week, and occasionally twice in one day, states that from taking regularly the Tincture of Sumbul he had obtained so much benefit, that from June, 1852, to the date of the letter, 16th of April, 1854, no epileptic fit had occurred.

A lady of rank wrote to Mr. Savory, that, through the persevering use of the simple Tincture of Sumbul, a young man on her estate had, from the very commencement of the treatment, been without a fit for eight weeks up to the 13th of November, and from that date to the 17th April (1852), he had again been quite free from attacks.

The dose of the plain tincture I recommend is from 20 to 30 drops, in water, twice a day, increasing five drops at a time up to a drachm for each dose.

Whoever says "Palsy of the limbs," says, possibly without knowing it, congestion of the cerebral mass, principally of the posterior part, foregone or present. I do not admit what is commonly called "weakness" to be the cause of paralyzed limbs ; yet it is a fatal error at the present day often committed. Hence the increased and increasing number of cases of paralysis that one meets, and sees, and hears of, even among comparatively young men ; and hence, also, the increased number of sudden deaths, which (paradoxical as it may appear) are increasing while the general mortality is decreasing.

In my Treatise on Sudden Death (1854), the materials for which I was collecting when the first edition of the present essay appeared,—the most ordinary reader will have been struck with astonishment at noticing so large a number of sudden deaths recorded in a comparatively short space of time among persons of consequence of both sexes, and between the age of forty and seventy. I have in that volume been able to show that such awful results were due to the fatal error of considering paralyzed limbs merely as the token of "weakness," instead of viewing them as shaking masts that have too much top-canvas, and to relieve which some of that canvas must be timely taken in, or the masts will go by the board, and the vessel be wrecked.

This increased frequency in the number of sudden deaths among the better classes of society within the last twenty-five years is truly striking. Among its many causes I reckon homœopathy, or the prolonged use of poisonous substances ; hydropathy, or the act of rudely interfering with the natural functions of the heart and brain ; also the burning of gas in sleeping apartments, lately introduced; and the mistaken horror of cupping, due to a most dangerous publication, entitled " Fallacies of the Faculty."

Within the last six years several cases of this pretended " weakness" of the limbs—treated as such, by means of tonics, chalybeates, high living, bitters, wines, &c., and all made much worse by such a method—came under my notice, some in the way of consultation, the rest simply as hearsay cases. In none of them was there any real weakness present, but the palpable necessity, on the contrary, existed for applying to Mr. Mapleson, to relieve the larger veins of the back of the head by the removal of a small (a small quantity is the most curative) quantity of blood. Where this was done, the pretended " weakness" of the limbs disappeared,—but that was only in few instances ; the rest of the sufferers would not hear of such a remedy as cupping, and they accordingly continue in the same state as before ; nay, two of them (both gentlemen under fifty years of age) have been gradually deteriorating, and are now arriving at that stage of the disease when congestion having spontaneously resolved itself at the expense of the soundness of the cerebral matter, real " palsy of the limbs," or genuine paralysis, that is, will supervene, in which such a remedy as the Sumbul may become of service, offering the best chance of recovery, unless softening of the nervous matter takes place.

The preparations of Sumbul suited to such cases are the substance itself reduced to impalpable powder, taken daily to from ten to twenty grains—increasing the dose cautiously as the case in its progress may require. Occasionally it will be found necessary to add a small quantity of the tincture, or the ethereal solution ; but care should be taken not to over-stimulate too much or too suddenly. To be safe in cases of paralysis of the extremities, the effect of the Sumbul should develop itself in exactly the reverse ratio of what is observed in the collapse of cholera, in which the salutary effect of the Sumbul is always, and must be, quick, or the patient will not recover; whereas in the disease under consideration, the reactionary effect of the Sumbul ought never to be quick, or the patient will run the risk of a fresh congestion in the head. Most people know that in cases of total loss of power in the lower extremities, the *nux vomica* has been employed with vaunted success. When so administered, that poisonous substance has restored motion to the limbs, by first producing jerks and subsultus in the muscles, as if galvanized. Precisely the opposite of this obtains when recovery of power in paralyzed limbs is the result of a careful and persevering employment of the Sumbul. The power of using them imperceptibly returns without the least convulsive or spasmodic starts in them; and whatever degree of such power is first obtained remains, to be added to by a second degree, due to a perseverance in the Sumbul, until, at length, the limbs are restored to their congenital power. With the *nux vomica* such is never the case. The jerks, or fits and starts, of the limbs under the influence of that drug are only transitory marks of returning power, which remains but for a short time, until reproduced by the same influence; yet there is no aggregation of small portions into one large and permanent measure of power.

I have thus contrasted the two modes of treatment, with the conviction that those medical men who have had experience in the manner of treating palsied extremities by the old remedy will be better able to determine how a treatment, based on the employment of this new medicine, may prove more satisfactory.

There is a case of this complaint under my care at present, in which the decoction of the Sumbul, and not the tincture or the powder, appeared to agree best with the patient, who now begins to stand, without support, on his legs, and even attempts a step or two forward without a crutch. My conviction is, that in the Sumbul we have a powerful agent for restoring motion and sensibility in all such cases.*

The Sumbul has been recommended with good results in some obstinate cases of what is called spasmodic cough, and I know it to be a most powerful agent in the early treatment of Diphtheria.

* The recovery in this case has since been complete.

My own experience in general dropsy has been limited, but so far seems to coincide with that of the physician of Darmstadt.

V. *The Sumbul checks Collapse-Cholera.—Account of the Russian Practice.*

Although the lapse of ten years, since this novel scourge has appeared epidemically among us, may encourage the hope that its future visitations will be few and far away; it will not be deemed incongruous that I should retain in this place the two following sections, as they appeared in the first edition. Nothing, to my knowledge, has transpired since which has not tended to confirm the statements herein contained, or the opinion I have herein expressed.

In the space of six months and three weeks, in 1848—that is, from the 4th of June to the 31st of December—22,022 individuals, out of a population of 445,000, were attacked with cholera at St. Petersburg, of whom 12,228 died; and at Moscow, between the 17th of March and the 14th of December, of the same year, in a population of 353,133, the attacks of cholera were 16,248, of which number 8025 ended in death. In the whole empire of Russia, during the same year, 1,686,849 were attacked by the disease, 668,012 of which proved fatal cases. There had been, therefore, 32,439 persons attacked with cholera every week during that year, of whom 12,846 died in the same time.

With such dismal statistics before them, officially announced in a report to the Minister of the Interior, it was to be expected that Russian medical men would apply themselves to the discovery of some better mode of treating that dreadful malady. This is what was done in 1849. Simultaneously with this research, an inquiry was instituted, in large hospitals and at the Academy of Medicine, into the pathology of the disease. Lastly, a more accurate description of the real genuine Asiatic cholera was drawn up from the careful and combined observations of eminent physicians. Unfortunately, their field for observation was too fatally vast, and they availed themselves of it.

While the inquiry into the seat and the real nature of the complaint was confided to the celebrated anatomist, Pirogoff—who, I observe by a recent number of the *St. Petersburg Journal,* has very lately published an " Atlas of the Pathological Anatomy of Cholera, in seventeen Coloured Plates, with a Text"—the merit of finding out a better mode of treatment devolved on Dr. Tillmann, chief physician to the very extensive civil hospital of Petro-Paulowsky, in St. Petersburg.

Based upon the result of upwards of five hundred *post-mortem* examinations, (some of which I witnessed during my last short visit to that capital,) Pirogoff came to the conclusion that there are two distinct seats of the disease: 1st, the intestinal canal; and 2ndly, the lungs; and he has further observed two kinds of intestinal cholera—the *simple* and the *mixed* —each offering different pathological lesions in the mucous membrane of the intestines.

On the other hand, very able physicians —such as

Arendt,Tillmann, Pellican, Rheinfeldt,Avenarius,&c. —whilst watching the very first onset of the disorder, its suddenness of invasion in individuals who had not ailed anything before, and the number of people brought into the hospitals out of the streets, where they had dropped down as if struck by a head-blow, had remarked that the suspension of the vital functions partook more of the character of that which is observed in asphyxia, or drowning, and came to the conclusion, that in all such cases (and they have been the most numerous as well as the most formidable in all the epidemics of cholera) the treatment ought to be the same as is used in those emergencies. They accordingly recommended—1st, a quick restoration of animal heat; 2ndly, an energetic remedy that should put and keep the heart in full action, even to the risk of producing cerebral excitement ; 3rdly, bleeding, if, by the two preceding means, such a full reaction should be produced as to give rise to head symptoms. The application of these views in practice I witnessed on the spot myself, and it was followed by success.

As the announcement of such a practice to the English public was first made by me in the letter addressed to the *Times*, twice before mentioned, and as on that occasion the Sumbul was first introduced to the notice of the medical profession in this country, it will not be inopportune to quote in this place a portion of that letter: it will form an apt completion to the chronological record of the introduction of the Sumbul into the materia medica of England. The letter, it will be recollected, was dated from the

Baths of Kissingen, a place I have been in the habit of visiting for the last sixteen years, and continue to visit professionally during the months of July and August, and part of September, to attend to the treatment of the several patients from this country who have recourse, under the advice of the London physicians or my own, to those remarkable waters.* I had just returned from attending a professional engagement to which I had been called in the Russian capital, and I thought that the very first and best use I could make of the valuable information I had there collected, respecting a novel treatment of the fearful disease which I knew was just then making great havoc in the metropolis of England, was to communicate it to my professional brethren through the most extensively read of the English journals.

"But there is a point in the Russian practice, equally novel, I think, which I desire to mention, and that is, the recent substitution of a vegetable substance, first recommended by Dr. Tillmann, chief

---

* I avail myself of this opportunity of contradicting a most unfounded report, which I have for the last two or three years found to prevail among many of my own old patients and strangers in London, as well as in the country, that I have relinquished practice altogether. How and with what view such a report has been started it is not for me to discover; all I may be allowed, in justice to myself, to say, is, that I have never absented myself longer than most London physicians do in the summer and autumn, and then always for professional purposes, and never for mere diversion. I trust the reader will excuse this egotistical note in my own justification.

physician of the Petro-Paulowsky Hospital, in lieu of the ammoniated or spirituous stimulants employed with the view of dispersing the state of stagnation of the blood and inward inanity. This substance was made known to me under the name of ' Sumbul,' said to be the produce of India, and to have in every case led to most surprising results. It may be given in substance, but it is more generally employed in the form of decoction or infusion, by spoonfuls frequently administered. Its power, however, in the way of reanimating the dying energies of a collapsed patient, has been found such as to demand great caution, lest it should produce cerebral excitement, and thence a typhoid fever—a consequence that has often been witnessed in the Russian hospitals subsequently to the recovery from the first or more dangerous stage of cholera.

" The taste of this singular drug (which in appearance looks like a mass of the roots and leaves of a greenish plant bruised and pressed together) is strongly bitter, and at the same time aromatic and exciting, the diffused impression continuing long on the tongue and throughout the mouth. I did not recognise it either by its looks or its name; yet it is, possibly, a well-known substance in the pharmacy of our own country. I have brought away a sufficient quantity of it to make a judicious trial of its virtues in our own epidemic," &c. &c.

" A. B. G.

" Baths of Kissingen, in Bavaria,
July 31, 1849."

The communication, of which the preceding quotation is an extract, detailed also the new and simple extemporaneous method of applying to a collapsed patient what is called in common parlance a *Russian bath*, which was found to recal animal heat to the surface of the body in a wonderfully quick manner; and it will be a subject of great regret if, after such an example, the English hospitals do not adopt the identical method, should, unfortunately, the Cholera again visit our isles—of which there can be but little or no doubt.

With the same communication, also, I forwarded to the *Times* certain official statistical returns of the progress and result of cholera in all the civil hospitals of St. Petersburg, from which it appeared that instead of the half of the attacked dying—as seems to be the general average everywhere, at the beginning and during the height of the disease—one-third only, or thereabout, fell victims to it in those establishments in which the new method had been perseveringly followed up. This favourable result the medical officers assured me they ascribed, and I think justly, to the action of Sumbul on the nervous system of the patients.

VI. *A Few Words on the question of Cholera.*

It would hardly be natural that I should suffer an occasion like the present to pass over, of expressing my own opinion on the subject of this ill-understood malady, without availing myself of it to the extent of the narrow limits I have prescribed to myself in this publication.

In a memoir entitled " Facts respecting the Nature, Treatment, and Cure of Cholera," published in the third and fourth editions of " The Catechism of Health," in 1832, on the first invasion of that disease in this country—the views I entertained of its essential character, its varieties, and the remedies which then seemed to me to be best calculated to check its ravages, were fully and plainly set forth.

The plan there suggested was to produce perspiration by the quickest and simplest mode possible —namely, the surrounding of the patient with a quantity of bran, or grains, just taken out of a boiler, the patient being at the same time packed up tight in blankets, as in the hydropathic system. This, with large draughts of hot white wine and water, or repeated draughts of warm water with the strong ammoniated drops, seldom failed to produce reaction and a profuse perspiration ; to such a degree, indeed, that, on a few occasions, it became necessary to have recoure to bleeding, by cupping or leeches.

Such a plan was adopted for the treatment of the collapsed cholera patients ; and it will be seen that, in principle, it is a plan analogous to the new Russian method of practice in the like case, as detailed in the preceding section. But the Russian method is the preferable of the two, in so far as it is more expeditious and energetic, owing to the novel means at their command—namely, the contrivance for instantaneously applying heat to the cold, clammy surface of the collapsed patient, and the new and powerful remedy so recently discovered, and which it has been the object of these pages to make more generally known.

Now, here is a well-defined, rational, and, as it has proved, successful system of cure, which the profession in two enlightened capitals have agreed to adopt and pursue during the last year's fearful epidemic to the exclusion of all the multifarious empirical suggestions and recommendations which, in all cases of universal plague, never fail to beset the reasonable physician. Here we have a tangible something remaining behind after the disappearance of the plague, which one can comprehend and look to as a sure resource for a future emergency of the same sort. Can we boast in this country of a similar result after our own protracted and most destructive plague, in which almost every individual medical man, no matter of what degree, has in his turn propounded, or recommended, or adopted, some one remedy, but never a regular and logically digested system of practice, to be followed by the rest of the profession? I apprehend that the answer cannot be in the affirmative; one reason of which is, that few or none of the higher classes have been attacked, or fallen victims to the disease—else we should have seen a more systematic and diligent inquiry into its nature and suitable treatment.

Cholera may justly be said to be the disease of the poor and ill-fed, as *influenza* is that of the rich and well-fed. Let the day-books of the physicians practising among the latter, either at the west or east end of the town, during the recent epidemics of cholera, be compared with their day-book during the great period of influenza in 1833, and it will be seen which period has given them most practice. Reverse the inquiry, and look into the ledgers of the general practitioners, or other medical officers appointed under the Board of Guardians and Commissioners of Health, to attend the poor, or who have visited the humbler classes, on their own account, during the corresponding periods, and it will be found that the one which gave them most employment was precisely that which had left the medical attendant of the rest comparatively idle. We shall find, in fact, on inquiry, that whilst the superior class of medical men had had, comparatively speaking, little to do during the cholera, the other class, on the contrary, had been overwhelmed with occupation, by day and by night, during the whole period of the epidemic. I entirely agree with the following exclamation of a correspondent and patient of mine, in allusion to the noble devotion and exertions of the class of medical men here alluded to : " I think the humbler *medicos* deserve being immortalized, and have shown the most noble absence of self." This very overwhelming occupation of the surgeon-apothecary, and comparative unemployment of the physician, may be considered as one of the main reasons for the little or no progress made in the investigation of the epidemic in England.

I do not hold the attempt made to fix the cause

of cholera to the agency of fungoid bodies, as propounded by Messrs. Brittain and Swaine, and supported by Dr. William Budd, of Bristol, to have been a step in advance towards the philosophy, or a proper knowledge of cholera. That theory, emphatically promulgated through the columns of the *Times* on the 24th of September, 1849, received its stunning blow within forty-eight hours, in the same journal, from the writer of these lines, and its death-blow a month later, in the official report of Drs. Baly and Gull to the College of Physicians. No other attempt or scientific endeavour of any kind was made, whether anatomical or physiological, during the prevalence of the disorder, to ascertain its real nature and causes, so that we might not be equally in the dark upon both subjects, as we have hitherto been, when again scourged by it on some future occasion. Is it not so ? I again ask : What have we gained in our late sad experience that shall serve us as a guide for the future ? Nothing.

I have purposely said, "nature and *causes*" of the disease, because a great deal has been advanced conjecturally in the public journals, and certain reports from official persons, upon both points, which would tend to lead us astray or confuse us in any real investigation of the subject. Thus, it has been asserted, among other conjectures, that cholera is nothing but an advanced state of diarrhœa—a complaint of the bowels, in fact, solely and exclusively ;—yet no farther proof than the mere coincidental presence of relaxation of the bowels, on the arrival of cholera in this country, has been alleged in support of such a

view ; whereas, where real anatomical and physiological investigations have been made, as on the Continent, the contrary was found to be the case.
There, every formidable symptom on the outset of
the disease, and every subsequent examination of
the fallen victims, have shown that we have to deal
with a far different affection in real cholera. That
we have, in fact, a sudden state of congestion and
coagulation in the larger organs—the brain, the
lungs, and the heart especially, produced by an epi-
demical condition of the air—which call for far different and more energetic measures than those
usually applied to disorders of the intestinal canal.

And as to *causes.* Much has been said of the
state of filth in which the poor live—their propin-
quity to permanent sources of fetid and noisome
effluvia—their want of good water—and, above all,
the foul condition of our great river. But these
writers forget that in capitals, such as St. Petersburg for example, where the cholera has committed
truly fearful ravages, especially in 1848, the most
magnificent river of living and limpid water rushes
at an impetuous rate through the city, unpolluted
by any foul additions ; and the police exercise the
most rigorous, nay, despotic influence in the preven-
tion of all the presumed causes of the disease above
enumerated. Upon this part of the subject, I could
proceed much further with my observations, did not
the limits of my present publication forbid it. One
only other remark, however, I am bound to make,
as more conversant with the circumstance, perhaps,
than the generality of my brother practitioners, and

c

that is, to point out the singular exemption or im-
munity which all localities possessing strong chaly-
beate springs have enjoyed during all the various
epidemics of cholera in Europe. We must not lose
sight of this *fact*, in our estimation of its causes.

Contagion also has been placed among the causes
of the rapid propagation of the disease. It is a
large question, which I have fully discussed in
another work, *ad hoc*, many years ago. From the
facts observed by myself, or learned from other writers
on cholera,—advocate though I have been, and am
still, for the doctrine of contagion in plague,—in
regard to cholera I came to a contrary conclusion,
and proposed, in 1832–3, to the Westminster Medical
Society, the resolution declaratory of their opinion
of the non-contagiousness of the disease, which was
carried ; candour, however, obliges me now to state,
that in a recent official report of the faculty to the
Minister of the Interior, at St. Petersburg, the
following words occur :—

"4. Le cholera se declarait dans les diverses
localités par *contagion*, à la suite de l'arrivée d'indi-
vidus qui avaient traversé les cantons infestés par la
maladie."

If, in point of therapeutical practice, we seem to
have gained nothing out of our late calamity ; in
point of hygienic views and prophylactic measures
we have unquestionably made a useful start, pro-
vided always that the start be seriously followed up
by the progressive and unremitting execution of
those views and measures. The present sanitary
movement will form an historical epoch in England

if it leads to all that it is capable of—the cleansing of the town—the purification of the river—the abolition of intramural sepultures—the extension of wholesome lodgings to the poor man—the universal establishment of baths and washhouses—the abundant and better supply of potable water — and, finally, the house-to-house visitation among the poorer classes, ere the distant cholera makes its stealthy approach to our shores. Lastly, the sanitary movement will be crowned with the fullest measure of success, if, when that formidable malady shall have again invaded us, we shall adopt the rational plan of treatment which the Russian bath and the use of the Sumbul present to us.

Dr. Reinsch, the distinguished physician and chemist, whose researches I have detailed, thus terminates his observations on that singular substance :

" I would have the physicians speedily to attend to the medicinal virtues of this plant ; for from its peculiar odour of musk, and its chemical peculiarities, its resinous principle, and astringent bitter extract, not less than from the remarkable quantity of starch contained in it, and its peculiar organization, we may justly conclude that the Sumbul must possess very peculiar properties, likely to operate beneficially on the human frame."

THE END.